BREAST CANCER

—Diseases and People—

BREAST CANCER

Janet Majure

Enslow Publishers, Inc.

40 Industrial Road	PO Box 38
Box 398	Aldershot
Berkeley Heights, NJ 07922	Hants GU12 6BP
USA	UK

http://www.enslow.com

Contents

Introduction to Breast Cancer

1

f breast cancer had a nickname, it would probably be fear. The disease stops even the most worldly women in their tracks. For example, television journalist Linda Ellerbee admits, "[The doctor] said, 'You have cancer.' He kept talking, but I didn't hear another word."[1]

Actress Jill Eikenberry's first reaction when her doctor recommended removing her breast, which had a small tumor, was, "'Get it off me.' I didn't know anybody who'd survived breast cancer."[2]

Feminist writer Gloria Steinem says, "I remember thinking, 'So this is how [my life]'s going to end.'"[3]

Years later, these breast cancer patients were alive and talking about their disease. Others, however, aren't as lucky. For example, in 1980 Liz Goldberg, a California woman, learned

she had breast cancer. She remembered her mother, who died of the disease at age thirty-eight when Goldberg was just eight years old. "You know how people say, 'You are just like your mother,' and they mean well?" Goldberg said. "Well, this little girl was thinking about breast cancer."[4]

These women are among the group of roughly one out of every eight American women who will get breast cancer sometime in their lives.[5] The disease is often difficult to talk about. There are several reasons. First, breast cancer is a complicated disease. That means there are not many easy answers. Second, it is a disease that can kill, and death can be scary to face. Third, the disease involves a woman's (or occasionally a man's) breasts. In our society this part of the body is identified with a woman's sexuality, and sexuality isn't always a comfortable topic. A child who participated in a support group for children in Toronto admitted he was embarrassed to talk about his mother's disease. "I wish it wasn't breast cancer," he said.[6] Just the same, Americans are learning to talk about breast cancer because it is such a major health issue.

Breast Cancer Is Common

Breast cancer is the most common cancer among American women, except for skin cancer. (Lung cancer, however, is the most common cancer killer among women.) According to the American Cancer Society, an estimated one hundred seventy-five thousand new cases of breast cancer would be diagnosed in 1999 among women in the United States. The society also estimated that about thirteen hundred new cases would appear

year. Then, from 1990 to 1995, the incidence rate has held steady at about 110.2 cases per one hundred thousand women.[8] The increase from the 1940s to the 1980s may be due to women's delaying motherhood and having fewer babies, which affects how many menstrual cycles they have. The number of menstrual cycles is thought to be a factor in developing breast cancer. Having a child before age thirty seems to reduce risk. Researchers don't understand why, but when a woman has her first child after age thirty, her risk is the same or slightly greater than if she never had children. The increase in incidence from the 1940s to the 1980s could also be related to women's increased exposure to environmental hazards, such as pesticides.

A surge in the number of cases during the 1980s is attributed to better detection due to the wider use of mammography. A mammogram is a special X-ray image that allows breast cancer to be discovered early in its existence. (*Mamma* is Latin for the word *breast*.) Once mammography became common as a screening tool, and early cases were routinely discovered, the incidence of breast cancer leveled off.[9]

Death Rates

Death rates from breast cancer stayed fairly steady from 1950 to the late 1980s. Between 1990 and 1994, the death rate fell 5.6 percent, which the American Cancer Society says is the "largest short-term decline in over 40 years."[10] The latest available figures, for 1996, indicate that the trend to lower death rates has continued.[11] Analysts say the decline is due to improved treatments and mammography.[12]

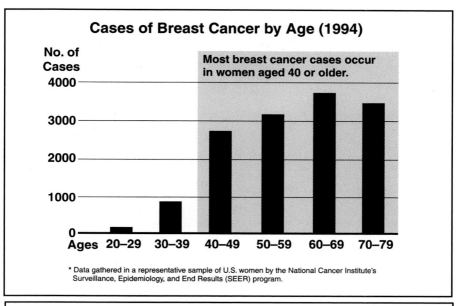

Cases of Breast Cancer by Age (1994)

No. of Cases

Most breast cancer cases occur in women aged 40 or older.

4000

3000

2000

1000

0

Ages 20–29 30–39 40–49 50–59 60–69 70–79

* Data gathered in a representative sample of U.S. women by the National Cancer Institute's Surveillance, Epidemiology, and End Results (SEER) program.

Odds of Contracting Breast Cancer (by Age)

By Age 30	1 out of 2,525 women
By Age 40	1 out of 217 women
By Age 50	1 out of 50 women
By Age 60	1 out of 24 women
By Age 70	1 out of 14 women
By Age 80	1 out of 10 women

Source: The National Cancer Institute's SEER program and the American Cancer Society, 1993.

These two charts show how a woman's chances of getting breast cancer increase as she gets older.

survival rate of similar people who don't have the disease. The American Cancer Society emphasizes that this relative survival rate is based on the treatment and diagnostic methods used years ago, before today's treatments were available.[19] That said, the numbers are still encouraging. About 84 percent of all women diagnosed with breast cancer survive their disease at least five years. The relative survival rate for all women diagnosed with breast cancer is about 67 percent ten years after diagnosis, and 56 percent fifteen years after diagnosis.[20] The breast cancer relative survival figures are based on actual population results, so they include all women diagnosed, regardless of what kind of treatment they received, if any.

Perhaps more meaningful are relative survival rates according to how advanced the disease is at diagnosis. As noted above, almost 97 percent of women survive at least five years from the time of diagnosis when cancer is confined to the breast. However, only about 76 percent of women live that long when the cancer has spread to surrounding tissue at the time of diagnosis. Only 21 percent of patients survive five years or more when the cancer has spread to distant locations at the time of diagnosis.[21]

Increased Understanding

Both the incidence of and death rates from cancer are getting lower. The improvement in women's chances of survival reflects advances in scientists' and physicians' understanding of the disease. However, there is still much to learn. Some women get treatments for breast cancer and never again have

2

What Is Breast Cancer?

Although breast cancer is common, women are still shocked and bewildered when they learn they have the disease. That was the case with actress Diahann Carroll. She didn't want to believe it when doctors told her she had breast cancer. She couldn't feel the lump that was visible on a mammogram. "I didn't want to deal with the reaction of others. I didn't want to leave my bedroom," she said. But her cancer was real, and she got treatment. Doctors removed the lump, and Carroll received radiation treatments for twelve weeks.

Even six months after completing treatment, Carroll said, "I'm just beginning to accept the fact that this is real." She also said, "There's no manual, no direction for dealing with this."[1] Like most breast cancer patients, she got lots of support from friends and a crash course in the disease. Although there may

Anatomy of the Breast

A woman's breasts are made up of breast tissue and fat sitting atop muscle. Here is how the breast is structured, starting from the chest wall outward:

The muscle that lies on top of the ribs is called the pectoralis. The pectoralis is covered with a layer of fat. On top of it is the breast tissue, then another layer of fat. Gelatin-like connective tissue holds the parts together. Skin covers it all.

The breast tissue consists of lobules and ducts. The lobules are clusters of milk-making glands, and the ducts are tubes that carry the milk to the nipple. Several sets of ducts and lobules are arranged in segments, like an orange. Each duct ends in its own opening at the nipple, but thousands of tiny branches extend out into each segment.

The breast tissue extends beyond the visible breast. The breast tissue goes from the collarbone to the lower ribs, and from the breastbone (in the middle of the chest) to under the arm. Blood vessels and nerves pass through the breasts, just as they do in other parts of the body. Lymph vessels also pass through the breast, carrying the clear lymphatic fluid that is part of the body's disease-fighting immune system.

The darker colored tip of the breast is called the areola. It includes the nipple, where the ducts end; little bumps called Montgomery's glands; sebaceous glands, which provide skin lubrication; and hair follicles.

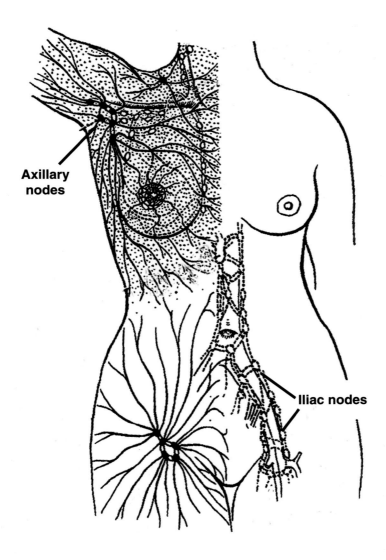

Axillary nodes

Iliac nodes

The lymphatic system is a network of vessels that carry the lymph, a clear fluid containing white blood cells that help fight infection and disease. Lymph nodes are scattered throughout the system. They help to filter the lymph fluid.

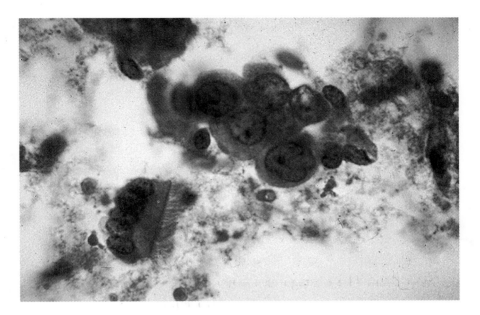

A microscopic slide of breast cancer cells.

occur that cause the cell to divide uncontrollably and spread, cancer develops.

When the cancer, or mass of abnormal cells, develops, it is undetectable initially, because it consists of just a few cells. Researchers estimate the cells will continue to divide and replicate for about eight years before they become detectable by mammograms. It takes about ten years for the cancer cells to develop into a lump large enough for a person to feel. By then, the cluster of cancer cells may be about one-half inch in diameter.

Untreated, the cluster of cancer cells, or tumor, in time spreads to other organs. This happens when cancerous cells break off from the tumor and migrate through the blood or

carcinogens, or cancer-causing substances, in the environment. For example, cigarette smoke is a carcinogen leading to lung cancer. No known carcinogen is a direct cause of breast cancer. Still, researchers have been able to find some characteristics shared by many breast cancer patients. (See Chapter 7.)

Certain specific genes have been associated with breast cancer. A defect in a gene known as BRCA1 has been identified as a probable cause of cancer. That gene, when normal, is thought to help correct DNA defects. Researchers estimate that 80 percent of women who inherit the defective gene will get breast cancer by the age of eighty.[2] However, only about 5 percent of all breast cancers result from this defect.[3] Other genes, including BRCA2, also have been identified as possible contributors to breast cancer. So far, however, there is no such thing as a single gene that controls breast cancer.

Knowing the Foe

Much remains to be learned about breast cancer. Researchers continue to seek answers. The more we know about the cause, the better researchers can determine and develop preventions and treatments.

Diahann Carroll is a good example of how recent medical advances have contributed to lower cancer rates. Through the use of mammography, her cancer was caught very early. Chances are strongly in her favor that she will survive breast cancer. In the meantime, she continues to perform onstage and to enjoy being a grandmother.

Former first lady Betty Ford, who announced she had breast cancer in 1974, was one of the first public figures to speak openly about her disease.

During the following centuries, mastectomy continued to be the primary treatment of breast cancer. It is likely that many women with the disease didn't seek treatment. When they did, their disease was far advanced:

> Instead, women suffered from glaring complaints, such as oozing ulcerations [open sores] and the malodorous [bad smelling] weeping of distended, deformed, throbbing, eroded flesh. Such agonizing symptoms, even more than [probable] death, caused the worst despair.[3]

During the Renaissance in Europe, from the fourteenth through the sixteenth centuries, advances in treatment consisted mostly of improved tools with which to perform the surgical removal of the breast. Among them were tools designed to hold the breast steady and away from the chest to allow a quick removal.

Later the lymph nodes under patients' arms became a source of interest. In the sixteenth century, famed French surgeon Ambroise Paré observed that breast tumors often affected the lymph nodes under the arm. Around that time, a Spanish surgeon named Michael Servetus first advocated the removal of the enlarged lymph nodes under the arm. Other surgeons of the period favored removal of the underlying pectoralis muscles, too.[4]

Eighteenth-century French surgeon Henri François le Dran first suggested that early breast cancer was a localized disease. He thought that the prognosis, or predicted outcome of the disease, was worse when it spread to the lymphatic system.[5] Those with early disease weren't eager for treatment,

Even with this new approach, the treatment did not often help. Halsted wrote, "The efficiency of an operation is measured truer in terms of local recurrence than of ultimate cure."[10] In other words, surgery eliminated cancer at the breast, but not the deadly metastases, the tumors growing in outlying sites.

Despite offering little improvement in a patient's life span, nineteenth-century doctors did gain some important knowledge. In 1842 in Italy, Domenico Rigoni-Stern studied death registries. He observed that the incidence of breast cancer increased with age and that unmarried women were more prone to the disease than married women.

In 1846 American dentist W. T. Morton first used ether as an anesthetic. In 1865 Joseph Lister, one of the most respected surgeons in England, showed that carbolic acid was an effective antiseptic. In 1867 he published papers on antiseptic methods. These developments soon made surgeries relatively painless and reasonably sterile. That meant far fewer patients died from infections resulting from their surgery. Still, it took decades for these methods to be widely accepted. Less helpful was the theory offered in France in the 1820s that having a sad or angry disposition increased a woman's odds of getting breast cancer.[11]

At last, some new treatments were offered in the 1890s, although they were little used at the time. In 1895 German physicist Wilhelm Roentgen discovered X rays. Two months later, according to some reports, Emile Grubbe, a second-year medical student in Chicago, used X rays on a patient with

administered tests, given to closely controlled and monitored groups of patients. Until then, doctors based their treatment decisions largely on theory and personal observations. The number one treatment by far in the first half of the twentieth century for breast cancer was a mastectomy. The surgery was appealing because it eliminated the tumor, even if it didn't cure the disease, as Halsted noted earlier. Systemic treatments, meaning treatments that travel throughout the body to destroy circulating cancer cells before they can settle into other organs, were not yet available. It took many decades for systemic treatments, such as hormone treatments or drug treatments, to become widely accepted.

Just the same, in the early 1900s some doctors began to question whether mastectomy should be used for all women with breast tumors. This questioning resulted in part from improvements in pathology, the study of disease and the changes in tissue caused by disease. Pathologists began to study the tumors removed from women's breasts. The pathologists discovered that mastectomies were being performed on women with relatively minor growths, such as ductal carcinoma *in situ*.

This observation contributed to efforts to study radiation treatments for small tumors in the breast. Radiation uses radioactive rays and involves invisible high-energy waves that can alter human cells. In 1898, Polish-born French chemist Marie Curie discovered radium, a radioactive element. A few doctors began to use it as an anticancer agent. In 1906, British surgeon W. Sampson Handley recommended inserting radon (a radioactive gas) tubes between the ribs in the sternum, or

breastbone, area to destroy cancer cells that remained there after mastectomy. In 1917, in New York, H. H. Janeway used radium between layers of tissue for women with breast cancer who refused surgery.

At first, radiation treatments were tried primarily on women with advanced cases of cancer. Often, the radiation slowed the progress of the disease, although the patients still died of their cancers. Still, this result established radium's usefulness in slowing the progress of the cancer. This discovery led Sir Geoffrey Keynes of Great Britain to introduce a new breast cancer treatment method. He combined lumpectomy (the surgical removal of a tumor plus a small amount of surrounding healthy tissue) with radiation treatment. In 1939, Keynes showed that the results of this combined treatment were as good as those for the radical mastectomy. Doctors rejected his treatment, however, evidently because the radical mastectomy was so deeply established as the "proper" treatment.[12]

In 1958, American researchers Bernard and Edwin Fisher began a series of studies. Their studies resulted in clear evidence that lumpectomy plus radiation was just as effective as mastectomy for women whose tumors were four centimeters (about one and one half inches) or less.[13] In 1990, the National Cancer Institute officially declared lumpectomy plus radiation the preferred treatment.[14]

Meanwhile, mammography, which uses X-ray radiation, helped identify cancers sooner in the course of their disease. Mammography was first studied in the 1920s, but its effectiveness for diagnosis was not proved until 1962.[15]

Naples' harbor. These sailors developed radically reduced numbers of bone marrow and lymph cells, doctors found. Someone had the idea that such a mechanism might work against cancer. Research then began on using nitrogen mustard to fight lymph cancer. Eventually, related chemicals were used to treat various cancers.[16]

Then, in 1955, researcher H. C. Engell reported that malignant cells could be found circulating in the bloodstream. This information was far from new; in 1869 an Australian named T. R. Ashworth had published a paper on the same observation. As was true in many other scientific developments, though, the first word was widely ignored. Engell's report, however, increased interest in possible systemic treatments. In fact in 1957, a group of scientists discovered 5-fluorouracil, one of the most important anticancer drugs.[17]

In 1956, the National Surgical Adjuvant Breast Project was created. It provided for the systematic study of various forms of chemotherapy. Since then, continuing research has added to chemical weapons against breast cancer.

A Revised View of Cancer

An early theory that breast cancer spreads through the lymph system is not complete. Now we know that breast cancer is spread through the bloodstream as well as the lymph. Today doctors know more than ever about breast cancer. However, they still have much to learn before deaths from breast cancer are . . . history.

Early Detection

Early detection is important. Today, it is estimated that 95 percent of women whose breast cancer is discovered early will survive cancer. Ideally, "early" means before the cancer has metastasized, or spread to other body parts. Unfortunately, doctors cannot tell for certain whether a cancer has microscopically spread. As a result, women need to identify any cancerous growths as soon as possible to minimize the chances of metastasis.

Most cancerous lumps are found in the breast or under the arm by women while bathing or conducting monthly breast self-examinations. A cancerous growth is usually at least one to two centimeters in diameter (the size of a marble) before it can be felt. Mammograms can identify cancerous spots less than half that size.

Occasionally, other symptoms can signal breast cancer. One of these is a bloody discharge from the nipple. Another is swelling or redness of the breast or dimpling of the skin that doesn't go away. Sometimes the nipple will turn inward. A rash or scaly skin over the nipple of one breast can indicate Paget's disease of the breast. These symptoms are rarely a sign of breast cancer, but since they occasionally can be, they should be checked promptly.

Screening for Breast Cancer

"Screening" refers to a test given to a healthy person in an effort to identify a hidden illness, in this case breast cancer. Here are the three chief screening methods in use:

Breast self-examination, or BSE. Women are taught to systematically feel their breasts at about the same time each month in order to detect any breast lump as soon as possible.

Professional examination. Women are encouraged to have a doctor, nurse practitioner, or physician's assistant physically examine their breasts at least once a year. Again, the purpose is to detect any lumps or abnormalities. The idea is that a medical professional has more experience examining breasts and may be better able to discover a lesion, or growth, that a woman might miss herself.

Mammograms. Mammography is the only screening method that has been scientifically established to reduce cancer deaths.[5] This fact has been shown for women over forty years of age. (It may also be true for younger women, but so far it hasn't been scientifically established.) Mammograms can show cancerous growths before they are large enough to feel. They can also show something called microcalcifications. These are tiny bits of calcium that appear as specks on the X ray. They may indicate the presence of cancer or a precancerous condition in the ducts.

Breasts naturally tend to feel lumpy, especially among young women. This lumpiness is thought to be related to the lobules' milk-making function. In a woman of childbearing age, the lobules are affected by the hormones' fluctuations during monthly menstrual cycles. The breast tissue is dense, and the breasts tend to get slightly fuller, more tender, and lumpier in the days before a woman's period, readying her for pregnancy. In women of childbearing age, therefore,

Breast Self-Examinations Are Important

The American Cancer Society recommends that women aged twenty or older do a breast self-examination (BSE) once a month. By doing so, a woman becomes familiar with how her breasts usually feel. That way, any change in the breasts becomes easier for her to detect. For a woman of childbearing age, the best time to do a BSE is a few days after her menstrual period ends, because her breasts won't be tender or swollen, as they may be before or during her period.

The recommended BSE method:

—A woman should lie on her back with a pillow under her right shoulder. She should place her right arm behind her head.

—Using the pads on the tips of the three middle fingers of her left hand, she should feel for lumps in the right breast. She should move her fingers over the breast in a circular pattern; an up-and-down pattern; or in a wedge, or pie-piece, pattern (where you start from the center and move outward, examining each "piece of the pie" in this fashion). Any of these patterns is fine, but she should use the same one each month to check the entire breast area.

—The woman then should switch the pillow and arm positions to the opposite side and check her left breast.

—Next, the woman should repeat the examination while standing. She could do so in the shower, since some breast changes can be felt more easily when the skin is wet and soapy.

—Finally, she should view her breasts in a mirror to look for any dimpling of the skin, changes in the nipple, or swelling.

If the woman detects any changes, she should see her doctor as soon as possible, even though most breast changes are not cancerous.

What is a Mammogram?

A mammogram is an X ray of the breast. In a mammogram, X rays are directed through the breast onto X-ray-sensitive film. This film is then processed like a photograph. A radiologist, a doctor specially trained in reading X-ray images, reviews the film for signs of cancer.

Technicians use a machine designed especially for taking breast X rays. The machine sandwiches the breast between two plates. One plate holds the film. The other plate presses down on the breast against the film plate. This pressure flattens the breast as much as possible during the time the mammogram picture is taken. The greater the flattening, or compression, the thinner the tissue becomes that is being X-rayed. The thinner the tissue being X-rayed, the more likely any possible danger signs will appear on the film. For a typical screening mammogram, each breast is X-rayed from two different angles, horizontally and vertically. Most women regard mammograms as uncomfortable but not painful. Modern mammogram machines use very low doses of radiation, about the same amount as a person would get from spending a day in the sun on a Colorado mountaintop.

When a Lump or Spot Is Found

When a woman or her doctor finds a suspicious lump, the woman needs to undergo further tests to determine if the lump is malignant, or cancerous. The same is true if a mammogram reveals a suspicious-looking spot. First, additional mammograms will probably be taken to get a better view of the lump or spot. A radiologist, preferably one who specializes in mammograms, will review the film.[8] Sometimes, a woman will get a sonogram. A sonogram is an imaging technology that uses ultrasound waves. It can show whether a spot is filled with fluid, like a cyst, or whether it is solid, like a cancerous lump or a fibroadenoma. A cyst is a fluid-filled sac and not a source of concern. A fibroadenoma is a benign (not cancerous) lump, most common in younger women.

If further mammograms, a sonogram, or both techniques fail to rule out cancer, the doctor will request a surgical consultation. The surgeon will then perform a biopsy. A biopsy is a removal of tissue by one of several different methods for the purpose of scientifically analyzing the tissue. A physician called a pathologist, one who specializes in diagnosing disease from tissues, then studies the biopsy sample.

There are several biopsy options. In a fine-needle biopsy, a doctor numbs the skin over the breast, then inserts a very thin needle into the lump and withdraws a few cells. A cytologist, a person specially trained in looking at cells, then studies the cells under a microscope for signs of cancer. If the lump cannot be felt, doctors use a special machine in combination with a mammogram or sonogram to locate the lump for a

biopsy. In either case, the operation usually lasts about an hour, and the patient does not need to stay at the hospital. New digital ultrasound equipment may reduce the need for biopsies by 40 percent.[9]

Biopsy Findings

The pathologist then analyzes the tissue and issues a report on the biopsy. About 70 percent of lumps turn out to be benign. However, some may indicate precancerous conditions. If the tissue is cancerous, the pathologist's report will give additional information about the lump that will help in making treatment decisions. The report will tell:

The type of cancer. The biopsy will reveal whether it is ductal cancer or lobular cancer, or one of the rarer cancer forms. It also will indicate whether the cancer is invasive or carcinoma *in situ*. Invasive cancer is cancer that has spread beyond the layer of tissue in which it originally developed. Breast carcinoma *in situ* is where the cancer cells have not spread beyond the duct or lobule. Some doctors consider carcinoma *in situ* to be merely a precancerous condition, not cancer itself.

About aggressiveness. Depending on the appearance of the cancerous cells, the pathologist will estimate whether the cancer is fast-growing (aggressive) or slow-growing. Other signs, including the presence of cancer cells in blood or lymph vessels, also give the pathologist clues about how aggressive the cancer might be.

nodes under the arm. Third is whether there are any signs of metastasis, or spreading. Breast cancer most commonly metastasizes in the bones, lungs, liver, or brain. Signs of metastasis include an open sore at the tumor site or enlarged lymph nodes above the collarbone. New bone pain, headache, or cough may also indicate metastatic disease.

Generally, stage 1 or stage 2 tumors refer to small tumors with no signs of metastasis and with lymph nodes that can or cannot be felt by touch (called palpable nodes). A stage 3 tumor is larger, with palpable nodes, inflammatory cancer, or with signs that the cancer has spread to tissues near the breast, such as the skin or the chest muscles. Any tumor with obvious signs of metastasis is considered stage 4. The stages are descriptions, not absolute definitions of the severity of a tumor. The definitions of the stages frequently change as researchers learn more about the disease.

Doctors usually conduct additional tests on anyone with a confirmed breast cancer diagnosis. These tests include a chest X ray and blood tests. A chest X ray may show signs of metastatic cancer in the lungs. A blood test can usually tell if breast cancer has metastasized to the liver. A test called a bone scan can identify likely metastases in the bones. If a bone scan shows a "hot spot," it is usually followed with another test. An X ray or a CAT scan (a short term for computerized axial tomography, another way to "see" inside the body) can often determine if the spot is cancer or something less severe. Less severe possibilities might be either a mending bone (a broken or cracked bone that is repairing itself), or arthritis, an

5

Treating Breast Cancer

For nine months, Mary Susan Herczog wrote about her experiences with breast cancer treatments. Each month from December 1997 to August 1998, the *Los Angeles Times* printed her articles. In the last article in the series, Herczog wrote, "If you are lucky, this is the way cancer treatment ends, not with a bang but a whimper." In her case Herczog received a combination of chemotherapy, surgery, and radiation. When it was all over, her cancer doctor, or oncologist, told her, "In my mind you're cured."[1]

Unfortunately, it wasn't quite that simple. It is always possible that a cancer cell has metastasized, or broken away and migrated to another part of the body where it lies undetected. That being the case, Herczog's "cure" didn't end her medical care. She began taking hormone treatments to reduce the

to help keep the cancer from coming back. Chemotherapy is a treatment for cancer using powerful drugs. These drugs travel throughout the body in the bloodstream. They are intended to kill any cancer cells that may have left the tumor area and migrated elsewhere in the body. Hormone therapy is treatment involving hormones. Most often, hormone therapy seeks to block the function of the estrogen receptors that many breast cancer cells have.

Complementary treatments might include prayer, meditation, acupuncture, and dietary changes, including the addition of vitamins and herbs. Studies have found that patients who use these techniques often fare better than other patients.[2]

Many doctors argue against so-called alternative treatments, however.[3] These treatments are unproved, and some patients use them instead of scientifically endorsed treatments. Alternative treatments may not help, and occasionally they can harm people. Worst of all, they may keep patients from seeking treatments that have proven track records.[4]

There is no single, standard approach to applying the treatments. In most cases, though, a patient receives a combination of surgery and a systemic treatment. Sometimes surgery is the first step. In other cases, a woman may receive radiation or chemotherapy before surgery. Radiation or chemotherapy before surgery often shrinks the tumor. A smaller tumor is easier to remove. Also, a woman's chances of preserving her breast, which is important to many women, are greater with a smaller tumor.

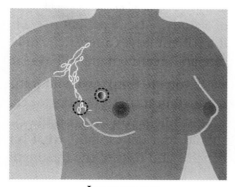

Lumpectomy

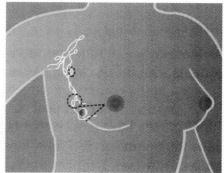

Partial or segmental mastectomy

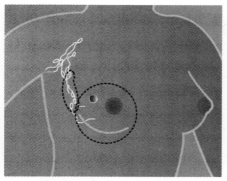

Total or simple mastectomy

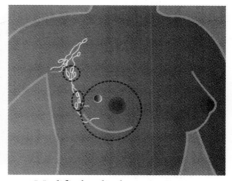

Modified radical mastectomy

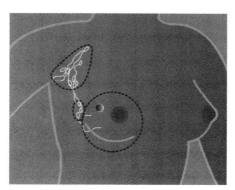

Radical mastectomy

These illustrations provided by the National Cancer Institute show the common types of breast surgery.

Breast Reconstruction

Reconstruction is the surgical creation of a new breast shape where the breast was removed. This treatment is optional. Some women prefer to use a prosthesis, or artificial breast form, in their bras after their mastectomy incision heals. Still other women accept their new, uneven shape.

Reconstruction can be done at the same time as the mastectomy. Women may also choose to wait until later to get reconstruction surgery. In either case, a plastic surgeon performs the reconstruction.

Reconstructions fall into two general categories: implants and natural tissue reconstructions. With an implant, the surgeon places an artificial breast implant under a chest muscle, secures the implant in place, and then closes the wound. The implant may be filled with saline (saltwater solution) or silicone. These are the same implants that are used for increasing the size of women's breasts. Because of recurring questions about their safety, silicone implants are used only in women who have had mastectomies and are willing to be part of scientific tests to determine the safety of these devices.

In tissue reconstruction surgery, a woman's own muscle, fat, and skin are transferred from another part of her body, usually the abdomen, to her chest and shaped into a breast. Surgeons can even create an artificial nipple with skin taken from other parts of the body.

Occasionally, the surgeon will do a subcutaneous, or under skin, mastectomy. In those cases the breast tissue and fat are removed from under the breast's skin and nipple. The woman's skin and nipple are then reused with the reconstruction.

been sunburned. Also, the skin in the treated area may become either more or less sensitive than it was before. When radiation is used with lumpectomy, the treated breast may feel firmer, or it may change size slightly. When the left breast area is radiated, chances of heart disease are increased slightly.

Chemotherapy Treatments

Chemotherapy is the general term for powerful drugs used to kill cancer cells. Chemotherapy is a systemic treatment, or one that affects the whole body. Chemotherapy attempts to stop

In addition to surgery, many breast cancer patients are treated with powerful cancer-killing drugs, called chemotherapy. Here a nurse selects a plastic bag filled with a drug treatment, which will be delivered to the patient intravenously, or directly into her veins.

Hormone Treatments

The female sex hormone estrogen fuels breast cancer cells' growth. Cancer cells that have estrogen receptors are particularly sensitive to estrogen. Hormone treatments are designed to counteract the effects of estrogen. These treatments aren't as effective for women whose tumors lack estrogen receptors, or are "estrogen-receptor-negative."

The most common hormone treatment today is tamoxifen, which is considered an anti-estrogen hormone. In a tumor, tamoxifen fills up the estrogen receptors, or docks, so that estrogen cannot attach to the cell. With tamoxifen blocking the estrogen from entering the cell, the cancer cell may die or shrink. Tamoxifen (brand name Nolvadex®) reduces the chances of cancer's recurrence. Tamoxifen has become a standard treatment for women with early stages of receptor-positive breast cancer. It is ineffective if the cancer is receptor-negative. It is taken in tablet form, usually for about five years.

Tamoxifen's side effects are more subtle than those of chemotherapy. A woman taking tamoxifen doesn't lose her hair or become nauseated. However, tamoxifen does affect other body parts and functions that are sensitive to estrogen. On the positive side, tamoxifen may reduce a woman's chances of having heart disease and osteoporosis, or bone thinning, especially among women past menopause. However, tamoxifen slightly increases the chances of blood clots and cancer of the lining of the uterus, called the endometrium. For women with receptor-positive breast cancer, however, the reduced chance of metastatic breast cancer outweighs these dangers.

is tied to the breast. A woman will learn to accept that the altered breast, reconstructed breast, or mastectomy scar will feel different from the original breast.

A woman also learns to deal with fear and worrying about whether she will remain cancer-free. She may wonder whether normal bumps are metastases. Doctors will show her ways to avoid lymphedema, which can develop months or even years after surgery. In addition, women whose treatments have provoked early menopause may experience unpleasant symptoms associated with menopause. These include hot flashes and night sweats.

For most women, though, the aftereffects are a small price to pay for the disappearance of their breast cancer. Even if their cancer eventually does come back, their treatments will usually extend their lives. The combination of early detection and current treatments means most women can live many years after their breast cancer is diagnosed.

him; Paul McCartney's mother died of breast cancer when he was fourteen.

Breast cancer can and does return in other parts of the body. In these cases, chances of survival are slim. Ninety-eight to 99 percent of women with metastatic breast cancer die of the disease. No one can explain why the other 1 to 2 percent of those women survive.[2]

"It could be a miracle, or good luck, or an extraordinary immune system," wrote Dr. Susan Love, a well-known breast surgeon and author. "Or it could be that the cells just go on lying dormant for an abnormally long time."[3]

Local and Distant Recurrences

Breast cancer tends to recur in certain places in the body. Some recurrences are local, meaning at the site of the original tumor. Others are regional, such as in the lymph nodes under the arm or collarbone. Recurrences elsewhere in the body are known as metastases or metastatic cancers. The lymph and blood systems are thought to be the avenues by which the metastatic cells travel.

Generally, local recurrences are treated as leftover cells from the original (or primary) cancer. In other words, doctors believe local recurrences are from breast cancer cells that the surgeon missed. These tumors may appear elsewhere in the same breast or in the scar from the original surgery. When recurrence is local, the patient is tested for metastases. She usually undergoes a bone scan, chest X ray, and blood tests for

not because I want to withhold information from my patient, but because I simply don't know."[5]

Treating Metastatic Breast Cancer

Treatments for a primary breast cancer aim for a cure. Treatments for metastatic breast cancer have different goals, since no known cure for it exists. Treatments for metastatic disease try to make the patient more comfortable. Treatments also try to help the patient live longer.

Treatments for comfort are known as palliative treatments. These are important to breast cancer patients. Although primary breast cancer is generally painless, metastatic disease usually includes pain. The good news is that doctors can do much to relieve this pain.

Specific treatments depend on the patient and the location of the metastatic tumor or tumors. (See page 70.) Breast cancer tends to recur in certain locations. The most common locations are the bones, lungs, and liver. Less common metastasis sites are the eye, the brain, and the bone marrow. Usually, symptoms of the metastatic tumors don't appear until the cancer has spread widely. Sometimes, however, periodic testing after treatment for primary cancer reveals metastases before symptoms appear.

Hormone Treatments

If a woman's cancer is estrogen-receptor-positive, hormone-related drugs are often the first treatment used in metastatic

disease. For those women, drugs such as tamoxifen block the action of the female hormone estrogen. Since estrogen in effect feeds this type of cancer, the blocking action of tamoxifen slows the growth of metastatic tumors. Women whose tumors are estrogen-receptor-negative sometimes can benefit from hormone treatments, but generally with less consistent results.

Doctors may also seek to stop the body's production of estrogen in women who have not reached menopause. Drugs, radiation, or surgery can stop the function of the ovaries. Ovaries produce most of the body's estrogens in a menstruating woman.

Other Drug Treatments

Many chemotherapy treatments for metastatic disease are the same as the systemic treatments for primary breast cancer. For a primary tumor, those treatments hope to kill any stray cancer cells. In metastatic cancer, chemotherapy aims to shrink tumors as much as and for as long as possible. Oncologists, or tumor doctors, have an array of chemotherapies to choose from. If one drug doesn't work, often another will.

Some chemotherapy treatments are largely reserved for metastatic disease. One of these is a new hormone treatment called capecitabine (brand name Xeloda®), which the federal Food and Drug Administration (FDA) approved in 1998. Tumor cells activate the drug, which then focuses on killing cancer cells. As a result, its side effects are less severe than those

Other Therapies

Sometimes, local treatments are used for metastases. For example, radiation may be applied to a tumor on a bone. The radiation will shrink the tumor and reduce the patient's pain. (See page 70.) Occasionally, surgeons will remove a metastatic tumor if it makes the patient more comfortable.

When local and systemic treatments no longer seem to help, pain medications can bring much relief. They will not prolong life. Still, they can make a patient's last months more comfortable. Sometimes, pain specialists can help when oncologists are unable to treat the pain adequately.

Emotional support helps prolong life. In one study, women with metastatic disease were divided into two groups. One group of women participated in a support group for one year. The other group of women did not. The women who were in the support group, on the average, lived twice as long as the other women.[11] Complementary therapies, such as meditation and prayer, also help many women feel better.

Saying Good-bye

For nearly all women with metastatic breast cancer, however, their disease ends in death. Eventually, pain relief is the only effective treatment. Many patients like to be at home with their loved ones in their final days. Linda McCartney and her family traveled to the Arizona ranch that was their retreat, and she died there. Others die in hospitals or in special facilities called hospices. A hospice is a place that provides care for

7

Breast Cancer Risks and Prevention

Susan S. Bailis has metastatic breast cancer, and she wants to know why. She also wants to know how to help prevent other women from getting it.

". . . I feel we have a moral obligation to our daughters to insist that scientists look hard for preventable causes of breast cancer," she wrote in *The Boston Globe*.[1] Bailis, a nursing home company executive, thinks substances in the environment might cause breast cancer. If such substances can be identified, then steps can be taken to eliminate the substances to prevent breast cancer.

Breast cancer prevention, however, has been a difficult goal. In fact, scientists so far have established only one method of medical prevention, the drug tamoxifen, which increases the risk of a different kind of cancer (endometrial). Studies

earlier, breast cancer appears to result from numerous mutations of breast cells. In fact, 70 percent of breast cancer patients have none of the known risk factors (except gender).[3] These risk factors include the following:

Gender. The number one risk factor for breast cancer is being a woman. Men get breast cancer, but a woman is one hundred times more likely to get it.

Aging. Although breast cancer appears in women of all ages, more than three fourths of cases occur in women over the age of fifty. More than half of this group of cases occurs in women over sixty.

Family history. When a woman's mother, sister, or daughter has had breast cancer she is more likely to develop it herself.

Genetic risks. About 5 percent to 10 percent of breast cancer cases result from inherited mutations of genes called BRCA1 and BRCA2. These genes normally help prevent cancer. Between 50 percent and 60 percent of women with inherited mutations of those genes develop breast cancer by age seventy.[4] Another gene, P-53, suppresses tumors. A mutation in it can increase the risk of developing breast cancer and other cancers. However, it is rarely a cause of breast cancer. Tests on blood can determine whether a woman has inherited any of these gene mutations. The American Cancer Society warns that these tests are expensive and may not be covered by insurance. Genetic counseling is recommended before undertaking the test. There are also concerns that a finding of a mutation may make it difficult or very expensive for a woman to get health insurance coverage.[5]

mammograms, today use very little radiation and are of far greater benefit than risk. When X rays were first used in the first half of the twentieth century, however, radiation doses were commonly much higher, and the dangers weren't known.

Diet and obesity. It's clear that diet affects cancer rates, but it isn't clear exactly how. Among the possible dietary culprits are excesses of fats, hormones in foods such as beef and chicken, and pesticides on or in food.

Alcohol consumption, especially in women who have no other risk factors. Women who have one drink a day have a very small increase in breast cancer risk. Women who have two to five alcoholic drinks a day are 1.5 times more likely to get breast cancer than women who don't drink at all.[6]

Taking Steps to Prevention

Many of the risk factors are traits over which a woman has no control. A woman obviously can't stop aging, change her family's history, undo a previous cancer, or do much to control how many menstrual cycles she has.

One thing a healthy woman can do that will reduce her risk is to quit drinking alcohol, or at least limit her alcohol intake to one drink a day. A healthy diet, low in fat and high in fresh fruits and vegetables, may help. Being physically active on a regular basis may also help. The exact role of diet and exercise as preventive factors is not yet clear, however, and continues to be studied. On the other hand, a healthy diet and regular exercise have been established as factors that aid a person's immune system. The immune system, which fights

cancer. Researchers estimated that without undergoing the surgery, sixty-seven to ninety of the women would have developed the disease.[8]

Chemo-prevention with Tamoxifen

Early in 1998, the first successful breast cancer prevention treatment was announced, but caution is still in order. Tamoxifen (brand name Nolvadex®), a drug used to hinder recurrence of breast cancer, greatly reduced the number of cancer cases among women with increased risk of breast cancer. (See "Success Cuts Study Short," page 82.) As we have seen, tamoxifen is thought to work by blocking the "docks" on breast cells that have estrogen receptors. Taking a drug to prevent disease is sometimes called chemo-prevention.

Like most other potent drugs, however, tamoxifen has side effects. Some are minor. The most serious are contributing to another kind of cancer and causing blood clots. During the test period that ended in spring 1998, thirty-three women in the tamoxifen-testing group developed cancer of the endometrium, or lining of the uterus, compared with fourteen in the group taking dummy pills, or placebos. Seventeen of the women taking tamoxifen developed blood clots in the lung compared with six in the placebo group. Also, thirty women in the tamoxifen group compared with nineteen in the placebo group developed blood clots in major veins.

The chance of these dangers is slight, and less than the chance of breast cancer for the women in the study. Nevertheless, the dangers dampened the excitement about the

test results. In 1998, Fran Visco, president of the National Breast Cancer Coalition, said, "[T]his is not a drug for the average woman. It's not the prevention that we've all been demanding."[10]

Adding to concerns are two European studies announced later in 1998 that found no real difference in breast cancer rates between placebo-taking and tamoxifen-taking groups. Women participating in those studies, conducted in the United Kingdom and Italy, were different from the women in the United States study. For example, all the women in the Italian study had had hysterectomies (surgical removal of the ovaries and/or uterus). The women in the British study as a group were older than the women in the American study. Also, the European test lasted six years compared with only four years for the American test.[11]

More research is necessary to make definite statements about tamoxifen's potential benefits. Still, many people are excited to know that breast cancer can be prevented, at least in some women. In time, researchers hope to identify other, better prevention methods.

increase funding for research. Breast cancer also figures into broader social issues. These include medical care for poor people, how insurance companies affect treatment, how society treats women, and how to protect people whose genes work against them.

Speaking Up in Care Decisions

Only in recent years have women been asked their opinions about how their cancer is treated. In the 1970s Rose Kushner, a writer, was an early advocate of doctors' seeking women's

Women demonstrate for more funding and research during a 1999 breast cancer advocacy conference held in Washington, D.C.

First Lady Nancy Reagan is a breast cancer survivor. She increased public awareness of the disease, which led to better funding for cancer research.

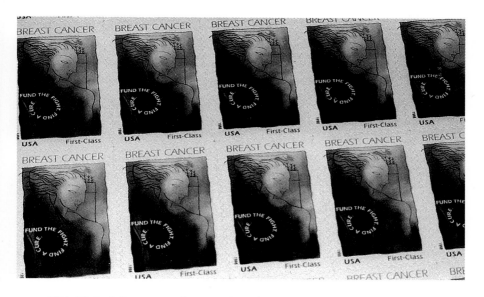

This United States postal stamp, issued in 1998, commemorates breast cancer and raises money for research. Each stamp costs forty cents, several cents more than the usual cost of a one-ounce stamp. The difference in price goes to fight breast cancer.

The Insurance Question

Health insurance is a major issue in breast cancer care. This is true for several reasons. Often, women who do not have private health insurance delay treating their breast tumors because they are worried about how they will pay the doctors and technicians. This delay results in reduced chances for a complete recovery.[10] Also, today doctors' recommendations about treatments are often subject to insurance companies' approval. This is a particular problem in cancer care because many cases don't respond to the standard treatments that are approved by insurance companies. As a result, doctors may recommend treatments that are still being studied. Insurance companies often refuse to pay for such as-yet-unapproved treatments.[11]

For many patients, the next step might be to enroll in a clinical trial. A clinical trial is a carefully constructed scientific experiment that investigates medical treatments. These trials are important for determining better treatments. Only 5 percent of patients, however, enter clinical trials. In 1980, about 80 percent of insurance companies paid for patients' care while they participated in clinical trials. In 1998, only about 50 percent did. Thus, fewer women get a chance at trying new treatments.[12] A new study found, however, that fewer than 10 percent of clinical trial claims are denied when studies do not include bone marrow transplants.[13] Insurance companies' decisions can be appealed, but the fight can be long, difficult, and expensive.

Women's Status in Society

It probably is not a coincidence that breast cancer "went public" in the 1970s. That is when the women's movement was in full blossom. Since the 1970s, women have raised their voices and their donations to cancer-fighting causes. The result has been increased awareness of breast cancer, greater social acceptance of its victims, and increased funding. The increased funding in particular holds out hope that better treatments will be found.

perfect methods and treatments for every aspect of breast cancer, from techniques of prevention and diagnosis to treatments for metastatic disease. Each new development holds hope for more breast cancer survivors.

Detection and Diagnosis

Early diagnosis currently offers the best hope for stopping breast cancer. Researchers are seeking more effective ways of detecting cancer. A new computer-aided system is being tested that appears to improve detection of early breast cancers. Now radiologists routinely review individual mammograms to determine whether cancer is present. However, occasionally, they overlook disease. The Food and Drug Administration estimates that twenty breast cancers are missed for every eighty discovered. Indications are that computer assistance may reduce that number by more than half.[2]

Researchers are looking into other technologies, too. One such method combines computerized axial tomography (CAT) scans with positron emission tomography (PET).[3] Studies have found that ultrasound (an imaging technique using sound waves) may also help in diagnosis.[4] Another test that measures electrical charges on the skin appears to be helpful in determining whether lumps are benign or cancerous.[5] One new imaging technique, called technetium tetrofosmin scintimammography, appears to be good for detecting cancer in dense breasts. Regular mammography doesn't perform as well when breast tissue is dense.[6] Also exciting is the preliminary finding that X-ray analysis of human hair can reveal breast

reasons. These regions include Cape Cod, Massachusetts; Long Island, New York; and Marin County, California.[11]

Other possible causes are being studied. These include the use of various hormone medications, such as birth control pills, fertility pills, and hormone-replacement pills for women after menopause. Also, weight gain, weight loss, exercise, and diet are all being studied.

Diet has gotten a lot of attention both because of the cultural differences in cancer rates (such as the differences between Asia and the West, or between rich and poor women) and because of a book issued in 1998 called *The Breast Cancer Prevention Diet* by Dr. Bob Arnot. Scientists and others have called the best-selling book "irresponsible" and a "disservice to women." Still, Dr. Moshe Shike, director of Memorial Sloan-Kettering Cancer Center's cancer prevention and wellness program, says, "We can say that diet in certain situations may help reduce risk. But we can't say it will prevent cancer."[12]

Nevertheless, other experts estimate 30 to 40 percent of all cancers, not just breast cancer, could be prevented by changes in diet and exercise.[13] Scientists are trying to learn the mechanisms involved. About ten studies have looked at the link between breast cancer and fruits and vegetables. Most of the studies have indicated that eating more fruits and vegetables can reduce the risk of breast cancer. The effect is slight, however.[14] Scientists hypothesize that weak estrogens, called isoflavones, in soy foods may help reduce cancer risk. If so, it's because the isoflavones, like tamoxifen, fill the docks where ordinary estrogen would enter cells. That theory has not been

Most studies have found that eating at least five servings of fruits and vegetables daily decreases one's risk of cancer.

The Pacific yew tree is the original source of the powerful anticancer drug Taxol. Now it is made synthetically in laboratories.

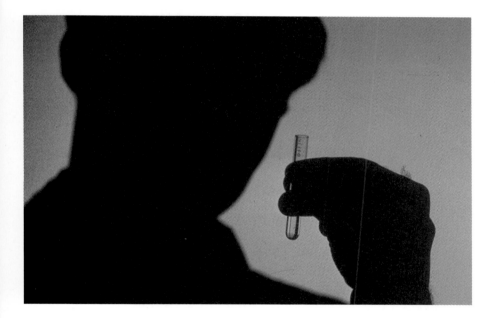

Researchers are always developing and testing new treatments that they hope will win the battle against breast cancer. One of these treatments is a vaccine that will help a person's immune system fight cancer.

Q & A

Q. I felt a lump in my breast, and I'm really scared. What should I do?

A. First, congratulations for checking your breasts. Next, see your doctor about it at once, just to be sure. However, if you are under age twenty-five, chances are less than one tenth of one percent that you have cancer. According to American Cancer Society estimates, only 4.5 percent of new breast cancers in 1998 occurred among women under age forty. Remember, too, that many young women's breasts are naturally lumpy. That's why monthly breast self-examinations are so important. Such regular checks allow a woman to become familiar with what is a normal inconsistency in the texture of her breasts. That way, any unusual lumps or thickening will be more apparent to her.

Q. At what age should girls start checking their breasts regularly for lumps?

A. The American Cancer Society recommends that all women begin monthly breast self-examinations by age twenty.

Q. How often should I have a mammogram?

A. Women under age forty should discuss this question with their doctor. Women from the ages of forty to forty-nine should have a mammogram and a breast examination every one to two years. Women over fifty should get a mammogram and breast exam yearly.

Q. My grandmother has breast cancer. Does that mean my mother will get it, too?

A. Not necessarily. However, your mother's chances of getting it are higher than a woman who has no relatives with breast cancer.

Q. I'm really worried about breast cancer. What can I do to prevent it?

A. First, be assured that most women never get breast cancer, so try not to worry unnecessarily. Unfortunately, no clear method of prevention is available at this time. However, you can reduce your risk by having a healthy lifestyle that promotes a strong immune system. Such a lifestyle includes regular exercise, eating plenty of fruits and vegetables (at least five servings a day), maintaining a healthy weight, and consuming no more than one alcoholic drink a day. Also, remember that the next best thing to prevention is early detection.

1962—Effectiveness of mammography was established.

1970s—Researchers identified hormone receptors on some breast cancer cells.

late 1980s—Breast health proponents began to use a pink ribbon as the symbol of breast cancer awareness.

1990—The National Cancer Institute declared lumpectomy plus radiation as the preferred first line of treatment for early-stage breast cancer.

1998—Medicare begins coverage for annual screening mammograms for women forty years and older.

1998—The first chemo-prevention for breast cancer, tamoxifen, was tentatively established.

cyst—a fluid-filled sac.

cytologist—a person who studies cells.

DNA—deoxyribonucleic acid. It contains genetic information on cell growth, division, and function.

duct—a tubelike vessel that carries milk from the lobules to the nipple.

estrogen—a female sex hormone.

endometrium—the lining of the uterus.

estrogen receptors—docks where estrogen links with cancer cells.

fibroadenoma—a kind of benign (not cancerous) lump.

gene—a segment of DNA that contains information relating to inherited traits, such as hair color and vulnerability to some diseases.

hormone—a substance naturally produced in the body, including estrogen, that regulates numerous functions, including the reproductive system.

hospice—a facility designed to provide a caring environment to help furnish the emotional and physical needs of terminal patients.

lesion—an abnormal growth in the breast.

lobule—a cluster of milk-making glands in the breast.

lumpectomy—surgical removal of an entire lump.

lymph—a clearing, circulating fluid that is part of the body's disease-fighting immune system.

lymph nodes—glands scattered throughout the lymph system that filter the lymph.

lymphedema—swelling that occurs when lymph fluid cannot drain properly; sometimes a side effect of breast surgery.

sonogram—an imaging technology that uses ultrasound waves.

staging—a system for categorizing tumor advancement.

systemic—affecting the entire body.

tamoxifen—the most common hormone treatment for breast cancer. Its brand name is Nolvadex®.

tumor—an abnormal growth of new tissue.

Susan G. Komen Toll-free Hotline
1-800-I'M AWARE

Y-Me National Breast Cancer Hotline
212 West Van Buren Street
Chicago, IL 60607
800-221-2141, 800-986-9505 (Spanish), 312-986-8338
Internet: http://www.yme.org

Internet Resources

Breast Cancer Net
http://www.breastcancer.net

Community Breast Health Project
http://www.med.stanford.edu/CBHP

19. American Cancer Society, *Breast Cancer Facts & Figures 1997–1998*, pp. 4–5.

20. Ibid., p. 5.

21. Ibid.

22. "Hope at Last," *People*, October 26, 1998, p. 68.

Chapter 2. What Is Breast Cancer?

1. "Victors Valiant," *People*, October 26, 1998, p. 62.

2. Susan Love with Karen Lindsey, *Dr. Susan Love's Breast Book*, 2nd ed. (Reading, Mass.: A Merloyd Lawrence Book, Addison-Wesley Publishing Company, 1995), pp. 187–188.

3. Vincent Friedewald and Aman U. Buzdar with Michael Bokulich, *Ask the Doctor: Breast Cancer* (Kansas City, Mo.: Andrews and McMeel, 1997), p. 7.

Chapter 3. A History of Breast Cancer

1. Harriet Beinfield and Malcolm S. Beinfield, "Revisiting Accepted Wisdom in the Management of Breast Cancer," *Alternative Therapies in Health and Medicine,* vol. 3, no. 5, September 1997, pp. 35–53.

2. James O. Robinson, "Treatment of Breast Cancer Through the Ages," *American Journal of Surgery*, March 1986, p. 317.

3. Beinfield and Beinfield, pp. 35–53.

4. Robinson, pp. 318–320.

5. Ibid., p. 320.

6. Ibid., p. 321.

7. Ibid., p. 322.

8. Ibid.

9. Ibid., pp. 322–325.

10. Beinfield and Beinfield, pp. 35–53.

11. Ibid.

12. Robinson, p. 327.

13. Beinfield and Beinfield, pp. 35–53.

14. Ibid.

4. American Cancer Society, "Alternative and Complementary Methods," <http://www.cancer.org/alt_therapy/overview.html> (June 29, 1999).

5. Cristine Russell, "Chemotherapy Endorsed for Early Breast Cancer," *The Washington Post*, November 25, 1997, page T7.

6. Herczog, p. 51.

Chapter 6. Cancer That Returns

1. Jeff Giles, "Lady McCartney," *Newsweek*, May 4, 1998, p. 65.

2. Susan M. Love with Karen Lindsey, *Dr. Susan Love's Breast Book*, 2nd ed. (Reading, Mass.: A Merloyd Lawrence Book, Addison-Wesley Publishing Company, 1995), p. 474.

3. Ibid., p. 475.

4. Ibid., p. 474.

5. Ibid., p. 484.

6. Gregory R. Mundy and Toshiyki Yoneda, "Bisphosphonates as Anticancer Drugs," *New England Journal of Medicine*, August 6, 1998, pp. 398–400.

7. Food and Drug Administration, "FDA Approves Xeloda® for Breast Cancer," FDA Talk Paper T98-21, April 30, 1998.

8. "FDA Panel Approves Antibody for Breast Cancer," Reuters, September 25, 1998.

9. Mary Brophy Marcus, "Tracking a Cancer Cure," U.S. News Online, June 1, 1998, <http://www.usnews.com/usnews/issue/980608/8canc.htm> (January 7, 2000).

10. Sjoerd Rodenhuis, Dick J. Richel et al., "Randomized Trial of High-Dose Chemotherapy and Haemopoietic Progenitor-Cell Support in Operable Breast Cancer with Extensive Axillary Lymph-Node Involvement," *The Lancet*, August 15, 1998, p. 515.

11. Ellen Gottheil, "Effect of Psychosocial Treatment on Survival of Patients with Metastatic Breast Cancer," *The Lancet*, October 14, 1989, p. 888.

12. Giles, p. 67.

3. Susan M. Love with Karen Lindsey, *Dr. Susan Love's Breast Book*, 2nd ed. (Reading, Mass.: A Merloyd Lawrence Book, Addison-Wesley Publishing Company, 1995), p. 516.

4. Ibid., pp. 319–322.

5. Susan G. Komen Breast Cancer Foundation, press release.

6. Love, pp. 521–523.

7. "Bill Would End Genetic Discrimination," United Press International, July 23, 1998.

8. Maxine S. Edwards, "Influence of Socioeconomic and Cultural Factors on Racial Differences in Late-Stage Presentation of Breast Cancer," *The Journal of the American Medical Association*, June 10, 1998, p. 1801.

9. "Blacks Get Worse Breast Cancer Treatment—Study," Reuters, May 10, 1999.

10. Arnold M. Epstein, "The Relations Between Health Insurance Coverage and Clinical Outcomes Among Women with Breast Cancer," *The New England Journal of Medicine*, July 29, 1993, p. 326.

11. Susan Brink, "No Miracles: A Family Fights Its Insurer for Experimental Treatments," U.S. News Online, June 8, 1998, <http://www.usnews.com/usnews/issue/980608/8canc.htm> (January 7, 2000).

12. Ibid.

13. Daniel Q. Haney, "Few Cancer Victims Test New Drugs," Associated Press, May 15, 1999.

14. National Cancer Institute, "International Range of Cancer Incidence," fact sheet. <http://rex.nci.nih.gov/NCI_Pub_Interface/raterisk/rates24.html> (December 9, 1999).

15. National Cancer Institute, "Cancer Death Rates Among 50 Countries," fact sheet. <http://rex.nci.nih.gov/NCI_Pub_Interface/raterisk/rates38.html> (December 9, 1999).

16. Love, p. 200.

15. Geoffrey Cowley, "Cancer & Diet," *Newsweek*, November 30, 1998, p. 66.

16. State University of New York at Buffalo, "Plant-Based Fat Inhibits Growth of Breast-Cancer Cell Line, UB Researchers Show," press release, April 29, 1999, <http://www.buffalo.edu/scripts/newnews/index.cgi?article=plantbase2> (December 10, 1999).

17. University of Wisconsin, Madison, "Compounds from Fruits, Vegetables and Grains Slow the Growth of Human Tumor Cells," press release, April 6, 1999, <http://www.sciencedaily.com/releases/1999/04/990406043901.htm> (December 9, 1999).

18. Mary Brophy Marcus, "Tracking a Cancer Cure," U.S. News Online, June 1, 1998, <http://www.usnews.com/usnews/issue/980601/lcanc.htm> (January 7, 2000).

19. "Decreasing Cancer Drug Dose Might Make It Safer," Reuters, October 6, 1998, p. 3.

20. Marcus.

21. Ronald Kotulak, "New Weapons Battle Cancer," *Chicago Tribune*, August 11, 1998, p. 3.

22 Ibid.

23. "Breast Cancer Vaccine on Trial," BBC Online Network, October 1, 1998, <http://www.bbc.co.uk/hi/english/health/newsid_184000/184192.stm> (December 9, 1999).

24. Business Wire, "NBC Featured Celsion Corp.'s Cancer System That Kills Tumors with Heat Alone on WRC Washington, D.C., TV News Channel," company press release, August 6, 1998.

25. Jennifer Arnold, "Seeing the Light," *Jacksonville Business Journal*, May 1, 1998, p. 25.

26. "Brave New Body," *The Washington Post*, August 25, 1998, p. Z10.

27. Kotulak.

Ries, L.A.G., C. L. Kosary, B. F. Hankey, B. A. Miller, and B. K. Edwards, eds. *SEER Cancer Statistics Review, 1973–1995*, Bethesda, Md: National Cancer Institute, 1998.

Articles

Bailis, Susan S. "Did the Environment Cause My Breast Cancer?" *The Boston Globe*, April 25, 1998, p. A17.

BBC Online Network. "Breast Cancer Vaccine on Trial." October 1, 1998. <http://www.bbc.co.uk/hi/english/health/newsid_184000/184192.stm> (December 9, 1999).

Edwards, Maxine S. "Influence of Socioeconomic and Cultural Factors on Racial Differences in Late-Stage Presentation of Breast Cancer." *The Journal of the American Medical Association*, June 10, 1998, p. 1801.

Epstein, Arnold M. "The Relations Between Health Insurance Coverage and Clinical Outcomes Among Women with Breast Cancer." *The New England Journal of Medicine*, July 27, 1993, p. 326.

Herczog, Mary Susan. "That Was Then, This Is Now." *Los Angeles Times*, August 10, 1998, p. S1.

Imperial Cancer Research Fund, "New Approach to Diagnosis of Breast Cancer Shows Promising Results." Press release, July 30, 1998.

Kopans, Daniel B. "Mammography Usefulness Does Not Change at Age 50." *The Breast Journal*, May–June 1998, pp. 139–145.

Kotulak, Ronald. "New Weapons Battle Cancer." *Chicago Tribune*, August 11, 1998, p. 3.

Lemonick, Michael D. "Beware This Breakthrough!" *Time*, April 20, 1998, pp. 62–63.

Index